FOREST
SINGER

To my son, Shamir Philip — S. S.
For all those I lived and worked alongside in Kitwe — A. A.

Barefoot Books
37 West 17th Street
4th Floor East
New York, New York 10010

This book is printed on 100% acid-free paper
The illustrations were prepared in watercolor
on Langton 300gsm watercolor paper

Graphic design by Jennie Hoare, England
Typeset in Cochin 16pt
Color separation by Unifoto, Cape Town
Printed and bound in
Singapore by Tien Wah Press (Pte) Ltd

1 3 5 7 9 8 6 4 2

Publisher Cataloging-in-Publication Data

Sikundar, Sylvia.
   Forest singer / written by Sylvia Sikundar ;
illustrated by Alison Astill.—1st ed.
[32]p. : col. ill. ;   cm.
Summary: Mabuti is a pygmy who lives in the forest with his family and
friends. Determined to stop them from teasing him about his singing,
Mabuti practices singing to the forest animals--and manages to tease his
friends in return!
ISBN 1-902283-60-0
1. Singing--Fiction--Juvenile literature. 2. Pygmies--Juvenile fiction.
I. Astill, Alison, ill. II. Title.
   [E]--dc21 1999 AC   CIP

FOREST SINGER

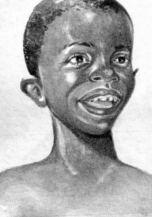

written by
SYLVIA SIKUNDAR
illustrated by
ALISON ASTILL

BAREFOOT BOOKS

Mabuti lived in a forest on the ancient slopes of the Mountains of the Moon in Africa. He was a Pygmy, and his people have walked the sun-speckled trails of that forest for thousands of years.

The Pygmies loved to sing and everyone, except Mabuti, would sing at any opportunity. They sang when they searched through the bushes looking for berries to eat.

They sang when they made a new camp in the
forest and built huts with branches and leaves.
They sang when they followed the honeyguide
bird to secret beehives bursting with sweet, sticky
honey. They sang when they gathered pearly
mushrooms from the rain-fresh earth. They sang
at night when the moon shone silver on the
whispering river, and fish leapt out from
rippling circles to catch fireflies.

The only person who didn't sing was Mabuti. When
Mabuti tried to sing, all his friends covered their ears.
"Did you hear a crow call?" asked one boy of another.
"No, I think it was a bullfrog, croaking in the pond,"
he replied.
"Or perhaps it was Mabuti," teased another boy.

Mabuti felt very downhearted. He wished he could sing like everyone else. He decided to go away and practice where no one would hear him.

He wandered alone through the forest and sang, but the monkeys in the trees chattered and shrieked at him.

"They don't like my singing," Mabuti cried, sadly. "But I'll keep practicing."

He rested by the river and sang, but the
basking crocodiles splashed noisily and slid into
the muddy water.

"They don't like my singing," cried Mabuti.
"But I'll keep practicing."

He sat by the hippo wallow and
sang, but the hippos groaned loudly
in protest.

"They don't like my singing," cried
Mabuti. "But I'll keep practicing."

CHILDREN'S ROOM

Day after day, Mabuti wandered through the forest trying to sing. Very slowly, his singing changed.

One day, as he sat under a tree singing to himself, a little dove perched on a branch above his head.

"Coo! Coo!" said the dove.

"Do you like my singing?" asked Mabuti, sounding very surprised. Then a pair of crested cranes circled overhead.

"Honk! Honk!" they called, as they glided to the ground.

"You like my singing, too," said Mabuti, feeling even more pleased with himself as he watched the two birds dancing gracefully in the sunbeams.

Then, in the far distance, he heard a
leopard cough.

"Grr Cough! Grr Cough!" called the
leopard.

"Grr Cough! Grr Cough!" mimicked
Mabuti.

After a while, the dove and the crested
cranes flew away, so Mabuti went down
to the river where the other children
were playing. He wanted to sing to them.

"Mabuti," shouted one of the boys, holding a large frog in his hand. "Perhaps this frog can teach you to sing!"

"I know how to sing. I don't need a frog to teach me," replied Mabuti.

"But he sings better than you do," laughed another.

"Maybe, maybe not," said Mabuti. "Let me sing to you."

"Oh, no!" cried all the children, as they quickly covered their ears.

Sadly, Mabuti turned and
walked away. The other
children were always teasing
him. Then suddenly he had
an idea. He would tease
them for a change.

He climbed into a leafy tree and hid in its
branches. He cupped his hands to his mouth.
"Grr Cough! Grr Cough!" he growled.

The other children stopped splashing and
stood silently in the water.

"It's the leopard," whispered one of the boys.
"He's coming to eat us."

"Grr Cough! Grr Cough!" growled
Mabuti again.

The children began to cry. "Please, leopard, please don't eat us."

"Grr Cough! Grr Cough! Sing me a song," shouted Mabuti.

The children sang a song about the forest on a misty morning.

"Grr Cough! Grr Cough! Can't you sing better than that? Is anyone else there?" said Mabuti, still pretending to be the leopard.

"Only Mabuti," cried the children. "He was here a few moments ago. He must be somewhere nearby."

"Grr Cough! Grr Cough! Let me hear him sing."

"He sounds like a bullfrog," said one of the children. "You wouldn't want to hear him sing."

"Grr Cough! Grr Cough!" said Mabuti, the leopard. "Let me hear him sing or I'll eat you all up."

"Mabuti," shouted all the children. "Can you sing a song for us?"

"I thought you didn't like my singing," answered Mabuti, in his own voice.

"Please try," begged the children. "Sing a song for the leopard, or he'll eat us all up!"

For a moment Mabuti was quiet, then he sang a song about the forest shining golden in the sunset.

"Grr Cough! Grr Cough!" said Mabuti again, pretending to be the leopard. "That was very good. Now I won't eat you all up."

Quietly, Mabuti slipped out of his hiding place.

"Mabuti! Your voice is beautiful," said one of the children. She was very surprised.

"I told you that one day I'd learn to sing," said Mabuti.

"It was so beautiful that the leopard didn't eat us all up," said another.

That evening, as everyone sat around the fire, his grandmother said, "Mabuti, I hear you sang a song today and saved the other children from being eaten up by the leopard."

"Grandmother," said Mabuti, "that's not exactly what happened." And he whispered something in her ear.

His grandmother laughed. "Now let's all hear your song," she said.

Suddenly everyone became very quiet, so quiet that they could hear the soft whisperings of the forest. Then Mabuti raised his face toward the stars and sang with all his heart.

Everyone listened in amazement.

"Those are the sweetest sounds I've ever heard," said his grandmother. "I'm sure that since the beginning of time no one has ever sung with such a beautiful voice."

Mabuti felt very proud. Now, whenever he walks the forest trails with his family and friends, he sings along with all the others.

Afterword

PYGMIES live in the forests of tropical Africa in the countries of Uganda, the Congo and Cameroon. In the past they obtained everything they needed from the forest, which provided them with food, clothing and shelter. The Pygmies have a great love and respect for their environment and sing many songs in praise of the forest.

Pygmies still live in small groups called bands. A band consists of several families who live together in a temporary camp in the forest. The men in a band hunt together to provide meat for their families. Some bands use nets that they make from vines. In others, the hunters use bows and arrows. The women and children gather nuts, berries, mushrooms, roots and other plants that they find in the forest. For some bands, caterpillars are a great delicacy.

Pygmies will stay in one place for a few weeks until the food supply dwindles, then they abandon their camp and move on to another part of the forest. When they find a suitable place, they make a small clearing and set up camp again. They use saplings to make the frames of their huts and cover them with large leaves that are overlapped to keep out the rain. Pygmies have few possessions and when it is time to move on, they must carry everything with them. The women often take the embers from the fire and use them to start a new one. In time, the forest takes over the abandoned camp.

Pygmies often trade or barter with villagers who live on the fringes of the forest. They give the villagers meat, honey and other products from the forest and receive luxuries such as spears, axes and cooking pots in return. They also receive clothing from the villagers but, when necessary, they can make their own from bark cloth. Sometimes they work for the villagers by helping to clear the land and tending to the crops, but unfortunately the villagers do not always treat the Pygmies well. Yet the Pygmies live in a way that is admired by more and more people because they do not inflict any unnecessary damage on their surroundings.

It is thought that the Pygmies have lived in the forests for over four thousand years, but their way of life is changing. Villagers are clearing more land on the edges of the forest to grow crops, and much of the Pygmies' traditional forest home is being chopped down for timber.

"The Mountains of the Moon" is another name for the Ruwenzoris, a range of mountains on the border between Uganda and Congo. The highest peak is Mt. Margherita, which is over 16,000 feet high. At one time, the Ruwenzoris were thought to be the source of the Nile River, but we now know that one of the major sources of the River Nile is Lake Victoria further to the east.

SYLVIA SIKUNDAR